Rub the page to release the smell-iciousnes P9-AGC-234

SWEET TREATS
SMELL-ICIOUS STICKER SCENES

Welcome to Shopville!
Are you ready for a smell-icious shopping adventure? Step through the doors of the Small Mart and use your scented stickers inside!

STICK A *Limited Edition Shopkin* IN EACH SCENE. CHECK OUT THE RIBBON ON EACH PAGE TO SEE WHICH ONE TO ADD!

Angie Ankle Boot Lee Tea Lenny Lime Rub-a-Glove Marsha Mellow Donna Donut

MEET THE SHOPKINS

Say howdy and get to know some of the adorably sweet characters that you will bump into in Shopville.

PLACE THE CANDY-SCENTED MINI STICKER FOR EACH CHARACTER!

TOASTY POP

Toasty Pop pops up when it's least expected, but she always has a warm welcome for everyone! The burning question is, what's her favorite type of bread? Toast, of course!

SNEAKY WEDGE

Sneaky Wedge is always running from store to store on a bargain hunt. She's footloose and fancy-free, but gets a little tongue-tied now and then.

MOLLY MOPS

Molly Mops is buckets of fun! She's a really hard worker, with a shiny personality. When it comes to finding a bargain, she loves to clean up!

DUM MEE MEE

Dum Mee Mee is no dummy when it comes to stopping tears. The only tears she likes to see are tears of joy when the sales are on!

JUICY ORANGE

She loves a juicy bargain and is always putting the squeeze on the shop owner for the best prices! Favorite color? Orange!

POPPY CORN

When it comes to shopping, no one does it butter! Poppy Corn really knows how to bag a bargain. She's first to the movies and last out, leaving a trail of popcorn wherever she goes!

CORNY COB

Famous for his corny jokes, Corny Cob can't help popping up to say hello when things get hot! And he's always happy to lend an ear!

OPEN FOR BUSINESS!

The Small Mart is the biggest shop in Shopville, and it's also home to the lovable gang of super-cute grocery characters, the Shopkins.

ADD SOME DELICIOUSLY SCENTED SHOPKINS TO THE SCENE!

Frozen

Bakery

LIMITED
EDITION
DONNA DONUT
Stick me in
the scene!

THE CHILLY OLYMPICS

It might be frosty in the freezer aisle, but Sneaky Wedge and her cool BFFs are keeping warm by taking part in the Chilly Olympics.

ADD SMELL-ICIOUS STICKERS, DRAW, AND COLOR TO FINISH THE SCENE!

YO-CHI

SNEAKY WEDGE

SPILT MILK

CHEEZEY B

SNOW CRUSH

LIMITED EDITION ANGIE ANKLE BOOT
Stick me in the scene!

HITTING THE FLOOR

When the doors of the Small Mart open each day, the Shopkins are shopping from 9 till 5. And after closing time, they have been known to boogie on down!

USE YOUR CANDY-SCENTED STICKERS TO FILL THE SCENE WITH SHOPKINS!

LIMITED
EDITION
LENNY LIME
Stick me in
the scene!

HIDE-AND-SEEK

There are lots of stacked bottles in the cleaning aisle—and lots of good places for Shopkins to hide! Molly Mops and Rub-a-Glove keep their eyes open for sneaky Shopkins in their section!

BRING THE SCENE TO LIFE WITH YOUR DELICIOUSLY SMELLY STICKERS!

LIMITED
EDITION
RUB-A-GLOVE
Stick me in
the scene!

MANAGER'S MEETING

The Shopkins keep the Small Mart open for business every day. Dum Mee Mee is holding a meeting to decide on some new groceries to stock in the store. What could they be?

ADD SCENTED STICKERS, DRAW, AND COLOR TO FINISH THE SCENE!

LIPPY LIPS

DUM MEE MEE

WATCH OUT!

Melons, oranges, and apples are rolling all over the floor in aisle 10! It will only take one Shopkin to miss their step and…SPLAT!

ADD STICKERS TO MAKE THIS SCENE SMELL GOOD ENOUGH TO EAT!

LIMITED EDITION
MARSHA MELLOW
Stick me in the scene!

TIME TO CHECK OUT

Use your smell-icious stickers to copy the picture of the Shopkins having fun at the checkouts! Check ya later!

Now give yourself five minutes to doodle as many groceries as you can think of on this page. Grab your shopping cart and start!

CART DASH

Once you shop you can't stop! Draw lines to help sort these mixed-up Shopkins into the correct baskets.

One of these Shopkins is from a different section. Circle it!

FRUIT & VEG

PARTY FOOD

How many of these items can you spot? Write your answers in the boxes.

Wobbles ☐ Carrots ☐ Shopping bags ☐ Green baskets ☐

SHOPPING SCENE

It's a busy day in Shopville! Use your chocolate-scented stickers to finish this busy shopping scene, and then answer the questions on the page.

Choc full of spotting fun!

Can you spot these little things in the big picture? Check them off.

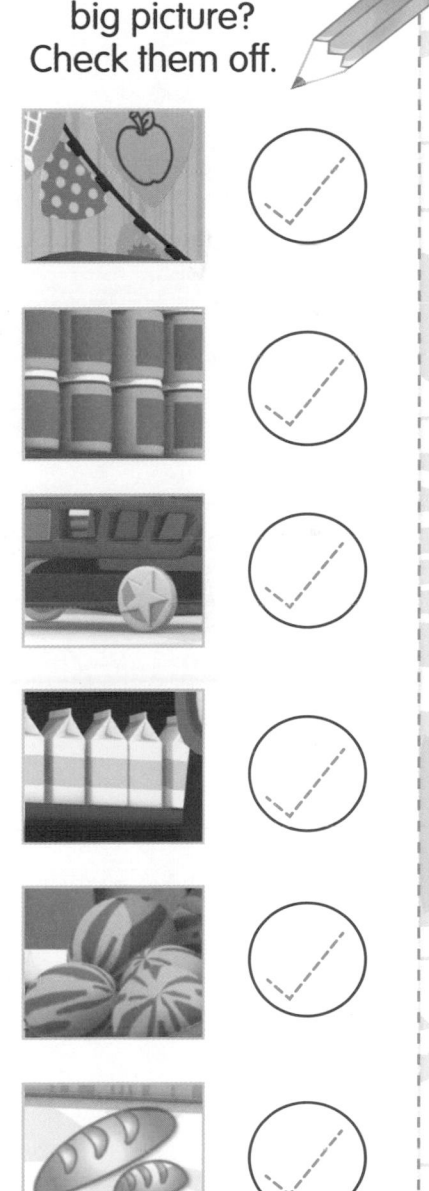

CHECKOUT CHECK

It's checkout time in the Small Mart! Look at the registers to figure out which Shopkin should come next in line, and then add your scented stickers to complete the patterns!

CHECKLIST

- SHAMPY
- SILKY
- SCRUBS
- POLLY POLISH

| Shampy | Silky | Scrubs | Polly Polish |

HEALTH & BEAUTY

CHECKLIST

- BREAKY CRUNCH
- GRAN JAM
- TOMMY KETCHUP
- PEPPE PEPPER
- SUGAR LUMP

| Breaky Crunch | Gran Jam | Tommy Ketchup | Peppe Pepper | Sugar Lump |

PANTRY

CHECKLIST

- POPSI COOL
- YO-CHI
- ICE CREAM DREAM
- SNOW CRUSH
- FREEZY PEAZY

| Popsi Cool | Yo-Chi | Ice Cream Dream | Snow Crush | Freezy Peazy |

FROZEN

STOCK-CHECK

Cheeky Chocolate is making sure that all the Shopkins are on their shelves. Use your deliciously scented stickers to add any missing Shopkins, and then check them off the lists.

CHECKLIST

STRAWBERRY KISS ◯
APPLE BLOSSOM ◯
POSH PEAR ◯
PINEAPPLE CRUSH ◯
MISS MUSHY-MOO ◯

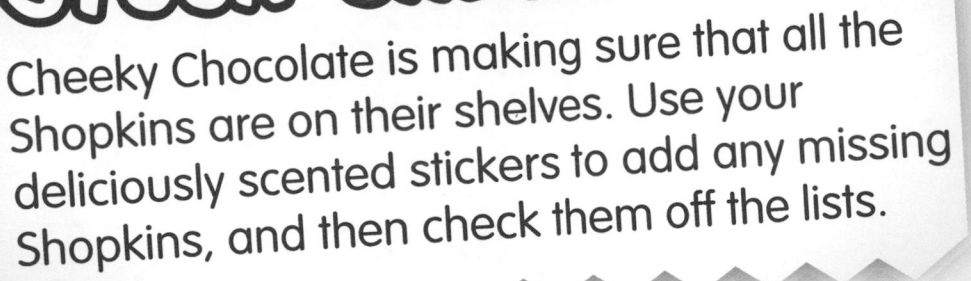

Strawberry Kiss　**Apple Blossom**　**Posh Pear**　**Pineapple Crush**　**Miss Mushy-Moo**

FRUIT & VEG

CHECKLIST

KOOKY COOKIE ◯
MINI MUFFIN ◯
D'LISH DONUT ◯
BREAD HEAD ◯

Kooky Cookie　**Mini Muffin**　**D'lish Donut**　**Bread Head**

BAKERY

CHECKLIST

SODA POPS ◯
WOBBLES ◯
RAINBOW BITE ◯
WISHES ◯
CHEEZEY B ◯

Soda Pops　**Wobbles**　**Rainbow Bite**　**Wishes**　**Cheezey B**

PARTY FOOD

TASTY TREATS

Color in these tasty Shopkins, and then decorate them with your sweet stickers to make them look (and smell) delicious!

My friends are as sweet as can be!

WORD SEARCH

There are lots of super Shopkins words hidden in the grid below. Can you circle them all?

M	S	H	O	P	V	I	L	L	E
O	Z	Y	N	A	S	B	U	S	V
S	I	T	U	S	H	C	Q	U	O
C	H	E	C	K	O	U	T	A	E
H	N	E	Q	T	P	K	P	O	B
O	H	O	C	V	K	B	P	O	A
C	D	F	A	X	I	K	U	M	K
O	A	R	C	K	N	Y	P	R	E
L	I	U	O	A	S	H	B	A	R
A	R	I	H	I	H	B	M	N	Y
T	Y	T	T	N	A	O	P	C	V
E	W	Y	Y	Y	E	T	R	A	C	T

SHOPVILLE   FRUITY

CART   CHECKOUT

SHOPKINS   DAIRY

BAKERY   CHOCOLATE

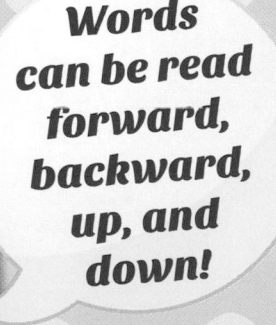

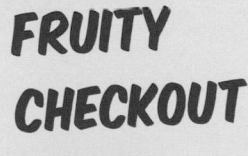

Words can be read forward, backward, up, and down!

BAG IT!

Which bag belongs to which Shopkin? Read the receipts, and then draw a line to match each Shopkin with their grocery bag.

CHEE-ZEE

1 CHEESE

2 BREAD ROLLS

2 CARROTS

CHEEKY CHOCOLATE

3 STRAWBERRIES

2 BREAD ROLLS

1 CHEESE

STRAWBERRY KISS

2 BREAD ROLLS

2 CARROTS

1 STRAWBERRY

MINI MUFFIN

3 STRAWBERRIES

1 CARROT

1 CHEESE

1 BREAD ROLL

A   B   C   D

CHEEKY COLORING

Place your Cheeky Chocolate-scented sticker in the box, and then color in the picture to match.

Color me sweet!

KOOKY COOKIE

Shy and sensitive, her friends are always encouraging her to "chip" in and try new things.

D'LISH DONUT

Super sweet but with a competitive edge, she's a HOLE lotta fun!

LIPPY LIPS

A sassy fashionista who's a little bit bossy. She definitely leaves her mark wherever she goes!

CUPCAKE QUEEN

LIMITED EDITION

So cute and sweet, she's one royal treat! This queen's rarely seen in public, but she'll bring a sprinkle of fun to any party.

MEET THE SHOPKINS

The Shopkins are the cutest collectible characters from all your favorite shops! Check them out and place your smell-icious Shopkins stickers on the correct shadows.

Come and meet my BFFs!

APPLE BLOSSOM

She's kind to the core and always up for a juicy adventure.

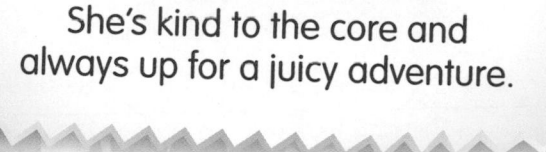

STRAWBERRY KISS

A fabulously fruity daydreamer with a huge imagination.

CHEE-ZEE

A confident and passionate performer who loves taking center stage.

CHEEKY CHOCOLATE'S
SMELL-ICIOUS STICKER ACTIVITIES

Hi, I'm Cheeky Chocolate!
I love hanging out at the Small Mart, playing pranks, and having fun with all my friends! Grab your smell-icious stickers and come with me on a Shopkins shopping spree!